THE CORONATION BALL

THE FOUR KINGDOMS AND BEYOND

THE FOUR KINGDOMS

The Princess Companion: A Retelling of The Princess and the Pea
(Book One)

The Princess Fugitive: A Reimagining of Little Red Riding Hood
(Book Two)

The Coronation Ball: A Four Kingdoms Cinderella Novelette

Happily Every Afters: A Reimagining of Snow White and Rose Red
(Novella)

The Princess Pact: A Twist on Rumpelstiltskin (Book Three)

A Midwinter's Wedding: A Retelling of The Frog Prince (Novella)

The Princess Game: A Reimagining of Sleeping Beauty (Book Four)

The Princess Search: A Retelling of The Ugly Duckling (Book Five)

BEYOND THE FOUR KINGDOMS

A Dance of Silver and Shadow: A Retelling of The Twelve Dancing
Princesses (Book One)

A Tale of Beauty and Beast: A Retelling of Beauty and the Beast
(Book Two)

A Crown of Snow and Ice: A Retelling of The Snow Queen (Book Three)

A Dream of Ebony and White: A Retelling of Snow White (Book Four)

A Captive of Wing and Feather: A Retelling of Swan Lake (Book Five)

A Princess of Wind and Wave: A Retelling of The Little Mermaid
(Book Six)

RETURN TO THE FOUR KINGDOMS

The Secret Princess: A Retelling of The Goose Girl (Book One)

The Mystery Princess: A Retelling of Cinderella (Book Two)

The Desert Princess: A Retelling of Aladdin (Book Three)

The Golden Princess: A Retelling of Ali Baba and the Forty Thieves
(Book Four)

The Rogue Princess: A Retelling of Puss in Boots (Book Five)

The Abandoned Princess: A Retelling of Rapunzel (Book Six)

FOUR KINGDOMS DUOLOGY

To Ride the Wind: A Retelling of East of the Sun and West of the Moon
(Book One)

To Steal the Sun: A Retelling of East of the Sun and West of the Moon
(Book Two)

FOUR KINGDOMS FAIRY TALE NOVELLAS

To Ensnare a Prince: An Entwined Prince and the Pauper Retelling
(Book One)

To Entangle a Heart: An Entwined Prince and the Pauper Retelling
(Book Two)

THE CORONATION BALL
A FOUR KINGDOMS CINDERELLA NOVELETTE

MELANIE CELLIER

LUMINANT PUBLICATIONS

*For everyone who remembered Hanna's story
and asked me where they could find it*

The Four Kingdoms
Northhelm
NORTHGATE
Arcadia
ARCADIE
Rangmere
RANGMEROS
The Great Desert
LANARE
Lanover
INVERNE

CHAPTER 1

*N*orthhelm *is a lovely kingdom.* I jerked the scrubbing brush back and forth across the long table.

You'll be happy here. A spray of suds flew into the air and landed on my arm.

They're a careful, methodical people. Who better to teach pastry making? The brush leaped from my hands and clattered to the floor. I leaned both arms against the table and sighed.

I knew I wasn't being fair to Northhelm, but I wasn't in the mood for fair. I wasn't being fair to my younger self either. I *had* been happy in Northhelm, once. And they *were* excellent at making pastries.

"Bad day?" asked a sympathetic voice.

I closed my eyes and took a deep breath, trying to let all the frustration drain away before turning to face my best friend.

"No worse than usual." I shrugged.

He hoisted himself up onto the freshly scrubbed table and bit into an apple he'd no doubt stolen from the pantry.

"I find that hard to believe." He paused for another bite. "You usually have a smile on your face. And that despite the fact that you're here at dawn with the first of them and always the last to leave. How many times have I found you here, all alone, doing some menial chore or other?"

He gave me a mock glare as if daring me to disagree. I said nothing.

"And so, I'm forced to conclude that something worse than usual has occurred. Come on Hanna, tell me." He patted the table beside him and produced a second apple from his jacket.

I looked around guiltily, but no one was in sight. The palace kitchens were dark and quiet; the other staff already resting before our usual early start.

I settled onto the table next to him and accepted the apple.

"You know, one day the head cook is going to catch you stealing these, and then you'll be in trouble."

Stefan grinned at me. "You know the cook has a soft spot for me. It's because I'm such a charming fellow."

I snorted. "It's because you flatter her so tremendously."

"Well, yes, that too." His laugh rang through the silent kitchens, and the last of my earlier tension slipped away.

Stefan always had this effect on me. It was one of the reasons I liked him so much. He wasn't the only palace footman who tried to steal kitchen treats, he was just the most successful at it. And he was the only one to regularly keep me company while I worked alone at the end of the day.

We munched in companionable silence for a couple of minutes while I thought about how different my years in North-helm would have been without him.

"It's Brianna, isn't it?"

His sudden question made me start.

I grimaced and reluctantly nodded my head. I didn't usually complain about work to him. I didn't see how it would help anything, and I knew that it made him feel helpless.

"That girl..." His vicious tone startled me, and I shot him a questioning look.

"I know you're too nice to complain about her, but she makes me so angry I want to punch something!"

I couldn't help laughing at him. He'd run a hand through his thick hair, and now dark locks were sticking up in all directions. It made his angry expression comical.

He caught sight of himself in a shiny pot hanging beside one of the stoves and made a face.

"I wish you'd let me help you." He vainly attempted to pat his hair back into place.

I was shaking my head before he'd even finished. "Of course I'm not going to let you get involved! Brianna may only be the daughter of a baronet, but she's still one of the upper class. You know perfectly well that people like us can't afford to anger people like her."

He shot me a sideways look I couldn't read, opened his mouth to say something, and then closed it again.

"I'm pretty sure you anger her just by existing," he grumbled after a moment of silence.

I wanted to deny it. My natural instinct was always to assume the best in people, but sadly his words rang true. I'd never done anything to antagonize Brianna, and yet she hated me anyway.

The worst of it was that the other apprentices followed her lead. In Northhelm, the crown valued practicality, and all younger children—even among the nobility—were expected to learn some sort of useful occupation. Even so, it had been a long time since someone as high ranking as a baronet's daughter had taken an apprenticeship in the royal kitchens.

She'd only done it because two years ago Master Girard had accepted the position of Royal Pastry Chef. He was the most famous pastry chef in the Four Kingdoms, and his prestige made the role more palatable. Plus, she wanted to impress her friends with her fantastic creations.

"Let me guess," said Stefan. "You were the one to bake that

incredible dessert the king and queen just complimented. The one Brianna was happily taking credit for."

"Wait, what?" My head shot up. "They served that? And the king and queen liked it?" A happy smile spread across my face, and I bounced slightly on the tabletop.

Stefan shook his head. "Of course you're not upset that she took credit. I should have known."

"I'm just so pleased they enjoyed it!"

"When have you ever baked anything that wasn't delicious?" Stefan patted his lean stomach. "I'm always being teased about the extra weight I've put on from sampling your desserts."

I rolled my eyes at him. Stefan was tall and muscled and didn't have an ounce of fat on him. And that was despite the prodigious quantities of food he consumed.

"Master Girard said it wasn't any good. He said he wasn't going to be able to use it. I've never seen Brianna look so pleased about anything. That's why I was upset earlier."

"What?" The word exploded out of Stefan, and I immediately regretted sharing the story. "That man is almost as bad as Brianna. I don't care how talented he is, he's an unfeeling monster if he can't see your value."

I shrugged. "You're forgetting that I came here from Rangmere."

It was easy to keep my voice light. I'd had two years under Master Girard to adjust to my disappointment. And even before that there had been others who felt as he did. My home kingdom had a bad reputation among the other kingdoms.

"And, even worse, you're a commoner!" Stefan tried unsuccessfully to inject a lighter note into his tone.

"Exactly."

"I still don't understand why you stay." Stefan sounded mutinous because in reality he knew the answer well enough.

"Yes, you do. I've dedicated five years of my life to this apprenticeship, and I have less than a year to go. I'm not leaving here without my journeyman qualification, whatever I have to put up with in the meantime. This is what I've always wanted to do. Plus, if I left now, it would break my parents' hearts."

"You still haven't told them, have you?"

I shook my head and tried not to look guilty. "I can't bring myself to do it. They would be so upset."

When I had been forced to flee Rangmere, my parents had followed and built a life for themselves in Northhelm. They had given up everything for me—even leaving my older brother, Hans, behind—and they were so proud when I was given the pastry chef apprenticeship. At the moment they were on their way back to Rangmere—their first visit to my brother since they left all those years ago—but I usually spent my free half day in the city with them. They loved to hear stories from the palace kitchens, and I knew they boasted about me to all their friends.

In the first three years of my training, it had been easy to find positive stories to tell them. The old pastry chef had been like a second father to me. He hadn't cared about where I came from or the social status of my family—he'd just seen that I loved baking as much as he did. He took me under his wing, fought to get me the apprenticeship, and taught me everything he knew. His death had been more devastating than any of my previous misfortunes.

A single tear dropped from my bowed head onto my wrist.

"Hey." Stefan lifted my head with a gentle finger under my chin. "You're thinking about Master Harman again, aren't you?"

"Sorry," I whispered, taking a deep breath to compose myself.

"Don't be." He pulled me into his side. "I hate how much your life has changed just as much as you do."

"It wasn't so bad before Brianna came," I said. "Master Girard didn't like me much, but he still let me bake. Now I spend most of my time cleaning and fetching."

"Someone should remind him he has three apprentices, not Brianna, Matthew, and a scullery maid." Stefan sounded ferocious, and a fresh wave of guilt hit me for complaining and dragging him into it.

He saw my expression and tightened his arm around me. "You're too nice for your own good. I know you need this position for now, but sometimes I worry that you've become so used to letting them walk all over you, that you don't remember how to stand up for yourself. Like right now, with everything you have going on, you're worrying about making me feel bad. That's the last thing you should be concerned about!"

I shook my head. "It's not worth making my life harder by provoking them. I just have to wait it out. And you're not going to convince me I should stop caring about your feelings. You're my closest friend."

For a second Stefan's stubborn expression lingered, shaded with something else I couldn't read, and then he sighed. "At least I can console myself with the knowledge that everyone else in the kitchens loves you. They haven't forgotten that you're always willing to go out of your way to help them. In fact, I snuck in here earlier to poach a bun and heard Girard telling one of the actual scullery maids to stay back and scrub this bench." He raised both eyebrows at me.

I ducked my head, embarrassed at being caught.

"The poor girl is sick and shouldn't have been working at all. The cook would have sent her straight back to bed, but Master Girard claimed he couldn't do without her assistance." I made a face. "That man is so self-absorbed, I don't think he sees anything beyond his own nose."

"Bravo!" Stefan gave me an extra congratulatory squeeze. "It's a relief to hear you not making excuses for the man—for once."

I rolled my eyes.

"And don't worry about Brianna," he added. "She's just jealous. She can't stand the fact that even though you're a commoner and a Rangmeran, you're still nicer, more talented, and prettier than she is!"

I couldn't prevent a small blush at his outburst. I hung my head, hoping to hide it in the gloom.

Stefan had never done or said anything to suggest he wanted to be more than friends. But sometimes, when I was alone in the kitchen, I let myself dream of a different sort of future with him.

Abruptly he released me, ran his hands through his hair again, and sighed.

"I'm sorry, Hanna. You deserve better than this."

"Well, it's not all bad." I smiled. "At least I have you to keep me company."

"Yes," he said, an unexpected frown on his face. "For now."

CHAPTER 2

*H*is last two words had been whispered so quietly I wasn't sure he had intended me to hear them. But I had heard them, and now I couldn't stop playing them over and over in my mind. What had he meant? Was he going away somewhere?

Despite my brave words, I wasn't sure I could make it through the last year of my apprenticeship without his encouragement and sympathy.

"*Hanna!*" Brianna's exaggerated sigh filled our corner of the kitchen. She had long since lost patience with my abstraction.

I turned around to find her glaring at me.

"You're supposed to be glazing these pastries." She gestured to several trays of prepared delicacies waiting to be placed in the oven.

I opened my mouth, then closed it again and reached wearily for the eggs. Brianna was the one who was supposed to be glazing. I had already spent hours creating the simple pastries, and the glazing had been the only task Master Girard assigned to her. But there was no point in saying anything. He was sure to take her side, regardless of the circumstances.

I had just finished the last one when Matthew came to collect the trays for the oven. His eyes darted between the dripping brush in my hands and Brianna who was watching me work with a bored expression. She raised her eyebrows at him, and he quickly smoothed the surprise from his face.

"Goodness, you're running behind," he said to me. "You're going to have to learn to move a bit more quickly if you want to succeed as a pastry chef." He looked at Brianna as he spoke and was rewarded with a broad smile.

"It's true," she said to me, her tone sickly sweet. "I was just thinking the same thing, but I didn't like to say anything. You might want to pick up the pace when you do the washing."

I ignored them and gathered all the dishes together. When I reached the closest sink, one of the scullery maids gestured for me to leave them with her. I shook my head and began to wash. Brianna would only be more unbearable if she saw me passing off the work to someone else.

The girl shot me a sympathetic look but didn't attempt to engage me in conversation. The maids had all learned that Brianna was a little more bearable if she thought I was miserable.

The whole charade was familiar, but as my arm scrubbed up and down in the routine motion, unwanted memories of Stefan's accusations the night before intruded. When had I decided I was willing to sacrifice myself so completely for the sake of peace? It had happened so gradually, I wasn't sure I could say.

The thoughts ran round and round in my head, but still my lips stayed closed, and my arm moved up and down.

I had finished cleaning up by the time the pastries came out of the oven. Master Girard appeared, apparently using the sixth sense that always informed him when baked goods were ready.

The three of us waited breathlessly as he sampled one of them. He took a long time to carefully consume all of the pastry before turning to us.

"A tolerable pastry," he said, and I had to suppress a proud smile. "The glazing in particular is excellent." He beamed at Brianna, and she thanked him with assumed modesty.

Matthew threw a quick glance at me, but luckily neither of the other two noticed. I had long ago learned to laugh at such ridiculous exchanges. I wondered if the glazing had really been well done. I was afraid I had skimped a little in my rush.

After a little more mutual admiration, Master Girard and Brianna swept out of the kitchen, accompanying the dessert on its way to the royal lunch.

Matthew and I were left to the uninteresting task of baking a seemingly endless number of bread rolls for the evening meal. We worked together for some time in silence until I turned around and discovered he had disappeared. A quick look around the kitchen revealed that he had gone to socialize with the cook's apprentices. I picked up my pace, knowing that Master Girard wouldn't be interested in any excuses if the rolls weren't ready on time.

As I worked, I once again dwelled on Stefan's mysterious parting words. Tears pricked against my eyelids, and I shook my head. Maybe I had misheard him. I was probably making a big deal out of nothing.

"Hanna! Hanna!" I was so deeply immersed in my thoughts that it took a moment to realize someone was calling my name.

I looked up in time to see one of the younger scullery maids nearly crash into my bench. She was breathing so heavily it sounded as if she'd run through half the palace.

"Have you heard?" Her dramatic entrance brought the other scullery maids hurrying over to find out what the excitement was about.

My first thoughts rushed to Stefan, but I quickly discarded them. Even if he was leaving, it wouldn't be of particular interest to the scullery maids.

"Out with it, Joanne," snapped one of the older girls.

Joanne's enthusiasm was unabated by the harsh tone.

"It's the earl and countess," she said, and I had to suppress a sigh. I didn't want to offend her, but I was getting a little sick of hearing about the Earl of Westforth's big ball.

Ostensibly, the ball was an opportunity for the Northhelmian nobility to celebrate the upcoming coronation of the new king of Rangmere—a gesture of respect and goodwill toward the neighboring kingdom. But the buzz around the palace suggested an altogether different purpose.

"About the ball for their son," she added unnecessarily.

Several of the other girls giggled behind their hands. Rumor said that the earl and his wife were throwing the ball to find a bride for their oldest son. The scullery maids thought it hugely romantic. I'd lost count of the number of times I had heard one of them murmur, "Imagine being chosen," over a sink full of dishes.

Not that anyone from the kitchens would be attending, of course—except for Brianna, as she loved to remind us. For the rest of us it just meant a lot of extra work.

Joanne was looking at me with an expectant expression, so I put as much interest into my face as I could manage.

"What about the ball?" I asked.

"Apparently someone told the countess that Master Girard has a senior apprentice from Rangmere. So now she and the earl have put in a special request that you make a Rangmeran dessert to be the centerpiece of the supper."

I stared at her.

"Really?" I managed to squeeze out, and several of the maids laughed.

A babble of voices expressed their delight and congratulations, but I was still in shock. This was the chance of a lifetime. All of the nobility from across Northhelm would be present, and if I could impress one of them, I might be offered a journeyman position in their kitchen. I couldn't rely on Master Girard to recommend me to anyone, so this might be my only opportunity to secure my future.

See, I thought at the absent Stefan. *This is why it's all worth it.*

But the thought of my status in the kitchens brought me back to reality.

"Do you think Master Girard will let me?" I asked the other girls.

Several of them looked hesitant, but Joanne shook her head.

"He can't refuse a special request from an earl. Especially not one as rich as the Earl of Westforth."

I considered her words, and my spirits lifted again. Master Girard's desire to impress the nobility was one of the few things stronger than his dislike of me. I began thinking about the different things I could make. It would have to be something impressive. Preferably something most Northhelmians hadn't seen before…

These new thoughts were much cheerier than my old ones, and they kept me occupied for the rest of the day. Master Girard appeared in the early evening and repeated the news. He emphasized that I would have to complete all my normal duties on top of the special creation for the party and added that it would be subject to his final approval.

"I won't allow anything inferior to be served at such an important function," he said.

I nodded dutifully, keeping the joy off my face.

My excitement helped me fly through the next few days. Between them, Brianna and Master Girard found an unending number of chores for me, but the extra energy allowed me to complete them with goodwill.

It even allowed me to block out Brianna's endless condescending comments about the ball and how fabulous it was going to be and how the earl's son was sure to fall in love with her. She particularly liked to emphasize the fact that the rest of us would be working but, thankfully, I was already good at ignoring her.

Every now and then I would catch the eye of one of the scullery maids and, depending on who it was, she would either roll her eyes or make a face. It helped to know I wasn't the only one who found Brianna ridiculous.

Whenever my tormentor realized I wasn't listening, she would sniff and make a comment about how she couldn't expect me to understand. What would I know about the nobility, after all?

I refrained from informing her that my best friend during my childhood in Rangmere had been Princess Ava. The information would just infuriate her, and I felt too happy about my baking opportunity to be bothered dealing with her anger. The ball had become a constant reminder of why I accepted my otherwise unpleasant situation.

My only concern was Stefan. I hadn't seen him in the kitchens since his ominous comment, and with each day that passed I became more concerned.

I was dwelling on his absence while I cleaned the kitchen on the third evening. Well, that and the exact dimensions of the pastry tower I'd decided to make. The last of the scullery maids was drifting off toward bed when I heard a familiar voice in the doorway. My heart leaped.

He was calling a cheery goodnight to the departing girl and within moments had appeared in front of me. My joy at seeing him spilled over onto my face.

"Now there's the smile I'm used to seeing!" He grinned back at me.

"Where have you been? I was starting to worry." I tried to sound annoyed but didn't quite manage it.

"Sorry." He looked genuinely contrite. "I've been so busy I couldn't get away. It's this stupid ball tomorrow."

He pulled a face, and I winced in sympathy.

"It's a lot of extra work, isn't it? I suppose you'll be on duty all night as well."

He sighed and ran his hand through his hair. "It's not the ball that's bothering me really. It's what comes afterward."

My mind instantly flew to his words from the other night. What was coming after the ball? I was desperate to ask but too scared to hear the answer. He was moving away—that had to be it.

Normally he was sensitive to my changing moods, but now his gaze locked on one of the large ovens as he appeared to wrestle with some thought.

His unusual distraction only fed my paranoia. I decided I couldn't bear the suspense after all. Closing the small gap between us, I put my hand on his arm.

"Stefan, what is it?" My voice was quiet in the large, empty room.

He looked down at my hand for a long time and then up into my face. I nearly stepped back in shock at his tortured expression.

"It's my family." The words seemed to burst out of him.

It wasn't what I was expecting—he never talked about his family. But perhaps they didn't live in the capital, and that was why he was moving.

"We have a..." He seemed to be struggling to find the right words. "A lot of people who look to us to take care of them. A lot of responsibilities. And my parents feel that I'm not taking mine seriously enough."

My mental picture of a distant family changed into an image of a large, dependent extended family somewhere in the city. Many young people were expected to use their position and income to support elderly relatives or younger siblings and cousins.

"After the ball, everything is going to change. I won't be able to come down here to visit you anymore."

"What, never?" My voice came out as a squeak. I tried to clear it. "Surely you'll still have some free time!"

"Yes, of course." His expression became even more tormented in response to my distress. "But I'll have...*other* responsibilities."

I stared at him, my face frozen. What did he mean by 'other' responsibilities? Was I just another responsibility to him? A charity case? Keep up the spirits of the poor, misused apprentice.

I whipped my hand away from his arm and stumbled back several steps.

"Hanna, no!" He moved toward me, closing the distance between us again. "That came out wrong. Believe me, I'd much rather be here with you. But I can't turn my back on my family or the people who need me. It's an impossible choice!" He ran both hands through his hair this time.

I took a deep breath. It didn't matter that my heart was breaking. If I truly loved him, I couldn't make this any harder for him than it obviously already was.

"Of course." I attempted a smile that came out a little twisted. "I understand. Your family and the people who need your support have to come first. I'll miss you, but I'll be all right without you. I'll finish my apprenticeship soon and be off to a new position anyway." I tried another smile, and this one came out a little bit more sincere.

"Oh, Hanna."

The softness in his voice made my eyes fly to his. The intensity I found there startled me. I would have stepped back, but his hands flew out and gripped my arms. He was standing so close now that I wasn't sure if the warmth I felt came from his body heat or mine. I began to tremble, but I couldn't seem to unlock my gaze from his.

"You're too good for me," he breathed.

His eyes flicked down to my lips as his head began to dip toward mine.

A soft clang from the other side of the kitchens caused his head to shoot back up. He released me and stepped backward, scanning the darkness.

"What was that?" His voice was ragged.

It had all happened too fast. I struggled to catch my breath.

"One…one of the cats." I felt barely coherent.

He relaxed slightly and looked back at me. The intensity returned, and then he groaned.

"What am I doing? I can't do this." He took one of my hands in both of his, and I tried to work out when his skin had become burning hot.

He bowed his head and pressed a kiss to the back of my hand.

"Goodbye, Hanna."

He was already gone from the kitchens before I fully registered his words.

CHAPTER 3

I arrived in the kitchens even earlier than usual the next morning. My nervous energy wouldn't let me sleep. Every time I closed my eyes, I could feel Stefan's breath warm against my face. It was, quite literally, a dream come true. Except that none of those dreams had ever ended with the word goodbye.

My emotions still hadn't decided if the whole thing had actually been a nightmare, and it didn't help that I needed to put all my attention into my pastry tower.

By the time the rest of the staff arrived, I had laid out all the ingredients and begun the initial preparations. Master Girard stopped to inspect my work but apparently could find nothing to criticize since he merely sniffed and moved on.

Brianna, on the other hand, looked far too pleased with herself. It made me nervous, but there was nothing I could do about it, so I kept working. By mid-morning I had almost forgotten about her. Focusing intently on my work had proven the only way to shut out the other thoughts racing around my mind.

The loud series of bangs that broke my concentration

attracted the attention of the entire kitchen. I looked up to see most of our work area covered in flour, broken eggs and broken dishes. I had never seen such a mess before.

Brianna stood in the middle of it, covered in flour and trembling with rage. She pointed a shaking finger at me.

"You, you clumsy *oaf*! How dare you!" Her voice rang through the shocked silence and brought Master Girard hurrying to her side.

"Look at what she did!" Brianna gestured to the mess all around her.

"Unacceptable!" Master Girard rounded on me. "You should have been more careful, Hanna. This is the worst possible day for your clumsiness."

I stared at him, too shocked to speak. I wasn't clumsy and still had no idea what had happened.

"You will clean up this mess and redo Brianna's ruined pastries before you return to your own work. Brianna will clearly need the rest of the day off to clean herself up and prepare for the ball."

"But…"

"I don't want to hear any excuses. If you value your apprenticeship, you'll do as you're told."

I snapped my mouth shut and watched him sweep Brianna from the kitchens. Just as they reached the door, Brianna turned her head and shot me a satisfied smirk. Everything clicked into place, and I suddenly understood her earlier satisfaction.

I gazed at the wreckage around me and then back at my own partially completed dessert. If I hurried, I might just be able to do Brianna's baking as well as my own. But there was no way I could fit in the cleaning as well. The task was as impossible as Brianna had clearly meant it to be.

I sank down onto the floor and put my head in my hands. I was too numb to cry, but I wasn't sure my legs could hold me. I couldn't do this, and my failure tonight would be as public as I had hoped my success would be. I would have no Stefan to see me through my final apprentice year, and likely no job when it had finished. What was the use of all my hard work now?

A nearby clattering brought me out of my self-pity. A bustle of movement around me took several moments to come into focus. Where had all these people come from? As my mind slowly refocused, I recognized the scullery maids moving purposefully through the pastry chef's section of the room, wielding cleaning cloths and brooms like efficient weapons.

They were cleaning up the mess Brianna had made.

I shot to my feet and held out my hands to stop them. "What are you doing?"

They already had double their normal workload due to the ball, so they had no more time than I did.

Talia—the girl who had been sick earlier in the week—met my eyes. "It was perfectly obvious you were nowhere near her. She's just trying to ruin your chances for tonight." She nodded toward my partially prepared pastries. "And we're not going to let that happen."

The other maids nodded in agreement. When I continued to stand there, too grateful to even speak, one of them nudged me.

"Well, hurry up then. We won't be able to do the baking for you."

My feet flew back toward my bench. "Thank you, thank you," I called over my shoulder.

Even as my hands resumed their work, my eyes met Matthew's. The apprentice was watching me with an expression I found difficult to read. I felt myself curl in, the weight of defeat pressing against me as I tasted my earlier despair. I had forgotten one of them remained behind.

Stefan, so present in my head, suddenly seemed to whisper in my ear. *I worry...that you don't remember how to stand up for yourself.*

I had told him I accepted my mistreatment as a temporary unpleasantness in pursuit of my dreams, not because I had grown accustomed to it. But if I let this moment pass me by, could I still make that claim?

I stopped work and put my hands on my hips. My eyes met Matthew's steadily.

"Well?" I asked, the challenge clear in my voice.

For a moment we stood there, our gazes locked, as something unspoken passed between us.

And then he shrugged, the tiniest of smiles lighting his eyes.

"None of my business," he said.

I smiled in return and got back to work.

With so many helping hands, the work and the afternoon sped by. My feet and back ached, and I hadn't stopped to eat, but the kitchen was clean and the baking done. I placed the last custard cream-filled pastry ball on the top of my tower and carefully drizzled the whole thing with melted chocolate.

When I stepped back to look it over, applause broke out behind me. I turned around to see the scullery maids and even some of the other apprentices clapping. I blushed.

"I just hope everyone likes it," I said.

"Of course they will!" said Joanne.

Footsteps approached from behind me, and the other staff scattered. Turning, I saw Master Girard surveying the kitchen and the completed baking in astonishment. He quickly hid his expression and turned a critical eye on my tower.

He took his time sampling the extra pastries I had made for that purpose, my held breath straining inside me the longer he took. When he actually smiled at me, I nearly collapsed.

"Better than I expected," he said. "It will do."

It was the highest praise I could remember receiving from him, and it made all the hard work seem like nothing. I felt so light, I could have floated all the way to the ceiling.

"If the earl and countess are pleased with your creation," Master Girard added, "they may call for the chef to present themselves at the ball. I advise you put on your best dress and cleanest apron, just in case."

I nodded and fled the kitchen before he could change his mind. The wings on my feet sent me soaring down the corridor, and as long as I was careful not to think of Stefan, excitement filled me to the brim. This was it! My big chance. Surely they would like it. I imagined appearing at the ball to receive their congratulations and thought I might burst, my insides pouring out like the custard from one of my pastry balls.

Most of the other staff had already left to help serve at the ball, so the kitchen was quiet when I returned. My tower was still there, in all its chocolaty glory, and the neighboring bench was lined with the pastries I had re-baked for Brianna.

I admired them all from across the room before catching movement out of the corner of my eye. Brianna was approaching the benches, and she didn't look pleased to find everything prepared and beautiful.

She had dressed for the ball in a gown of dark gold with a wide skirt. She looked even more out of place than usual in the kitchen, her hair piled on top of her head in an elaborate design. But even more out of place was the coal scuttle she gripped in one hand, her other hand holding her skirts well away from her dirty burden.

I couldn't understand what she was doing, but a presentiment of danger sent me hurrying across the room.

I wasn't fast enough.

As I rounded the last bench, she tipped up the scuttle and poured ashes from the fireplace all over the pastries I had re-baked.

"Brianna!" I poured my years of frustration into the scream, my earlier boldness with Matthew having unleashed my restraint. But she simply turned and tossed the last of the cinders over me.

I coughed, wiping my eyes so I could stare down in dismay at my once white apron. I wanted to scream again, raging and lashing out, but my momentary defiance had leaked away. I couldn't seem to muster anything but exhaustion.

"Why?" I asked at last, looking up to meet her eyes. "What did I ever do to you?"

"It's not what you did," she said, her voice filled with venom. "It's who you are. And I would have been willing to overlook that if it wasn't for your sneaky, deceitful ways. I saw you last night. I left something in the kitchens and came back to find it after everyone had gone."

My mind flew back to the night before, and I blushed underneath the ashes streaked across my face. Most of the footmen who lingered in the kitchens showed Brianna deference and admiration. There had been one—Justin—who used to show an interest in me a long time ago, but after Brianna arrived, he had quickly lost interest. And for once I had been grateful to her. I hadn't liked turning around at unexpected moments to find him watching me. Did she resent that Stefan hadn't gravitated to her in the same manner, stubbornly maintaining his friendship with me?

My brow creased. Now that I thought about it, I couldn't actually remember Stefan and Brianna interacting in any way at all. Had she even known of our friendship? He didn't tend to show up when she was around. He had once muttered darkly about only having so much self-control, and I had tried to avoid bringing her up around him after that.

"I saw you with my own eyes," she said, "so don't even try to deny it. I *will* be the Countess of Westforth, and I'm not going to let someone like you get in my way."

She looked crazed, her face transformed by rage, and I wondered if she'd gone mad. I'd always thought it unlikely that the earl and countess would choose Brianna as their son's bride, but I couldn't see how it had anything to do with me.

"What are you talking about?"

"I already told you not to bother denying it. I saw you in here, dallying with him. The whole thing is ridiculous. An earl's son and a pastry chef's apprentice. You make me laugh." She looked more like she wanted to rip my throat out than laugh, but I was too shocked to say anything.

"Once they've announced our betrothal," she continued, "I'll be making sure he never comes near the kitchens again. I don't know what you were planning, but it isn't going to work."

"It was dark," I managed to stammer, "you must have been confused. It was only Stefan…"

"Oh, *Stefan*, is it? From a common apprentice! That's Lord Westruther to you."

I stared at her. Lord Westruther was the eldest son of the Earl of Westforth. Clearly there was some kind of mistake.

I wanted to protest further, but several things were suddenly becoming clear. His family responsibilities. Why everything would change after the ball.

But he'd said he was a footman.

Or had he? I tried to remember if he'd ever actually said anything specific about his occupation. There were always footmen sneaking in after food, and I'd just assumed…

But how could it be true? Stefan—an earl's son.

He'd never dressed like nobility. But then I'd seen some of the noblemen in training gear before, and it did look remarkably like the off-duty clothes of the male servants. Northhelmian practicality again.

Then why had none of the other staff said anything? Of course, scullery maids hardly had the chance to observe the nobility. Maybe the ones who'd seen him in the kitchens hadn't known who he was either. And the cook had always treated him more like a favored nephew than a pesky underling. His avoidance of Brianna suddenly took on new meaning.

She seemed to take my stunned silence as capitulation because she turned to sweep away, dropping the coal scuttle at my feet as she skirted the black powder now coating my patch of floor. She'd barely made it a few steps, however, when Master Girard appeared.

His eyes flew from the ruined pastries to me and then down to the scuttle at my feet. He seemed to swell with wrath, his face turning purple as he struggled to form words.

"This…is…unacceptable," he finally managed to force out.

Brianna turned to look at me, all trace of anger gone from her face.

"She tripped," she said, her voice full of faux sympathy.

I had a sudden desperate longing to run over and smear ashes down her dress. I barely managed to suppress it. Such behavior could hardly improve my current situation.

Master Girard took several deep breaths and shook his head.

"Tripped? Tripped? I already gave you one chance today, girl. This is too much." He mopped at his forehead. "I notice you managed to avoid your pastry tower. Well, don't be thinking it will do you any good. There's no way I'm going to let you parade yourself in front of the nobility now." He stopped and had a good look at me. "As if you even could, looking like that!"

I opened my mouth to say something, although I wasn't sure what, but he rushed on. "As far as any of them are concerned, I made the dessert with the assistance of my one *useful* apprentice."

He glared at me, but my horror had bound me again in my old passivity. No appropriate words of protest formed when I needed them now.

Brianna, on the other hand, was practically purring.

"You can count on me," she said to Master Girard. "I won't let anything else go wrong. I'll serve it with my own hands."

Without doubt she would—to the earl and his family. I

somehow imagined the rest of the guests would find themselves beneath her notice, however.

I stood frozen in place, as if the soot was sticky as well as dirty, while I watched my dessert carefully carried out of the kitchen. Both my brain and my emotions were so overloaded that they had ceased to function.

But Brianna, the last to leave, swept a satisfied glance around the room, galvanizing me back into action. I ran forward and grabbed her arm.

She squealed at the sight of the black marks I left on her skin and pushed me away.

"You may be taking credit for my work," I said, my voice low, "but you won't be able to take Stefan. He'll never choose you. He hates you!"

If I had thought she was enraged before, it was nothing to how she looked at this pronouncement. But, instead of attacking me, she reached into her dress and pulled out a small clear bottle.

"Didn't you hear?" she asked. "I'll be serving Lord Westruther with my own hands. A few drops of this, and he'll forget you—or anyone else—ever existed."

"What…what's that?" I asked, thrown off by her tone of triumph.

"Only a little potion someone managed to…acquire…from one of the godmothers. I had to make a bargain with a very strange man to get my hands on it, but it was well worth it." Her smile of satisfaction grew. "After tonight I'll be done with these kitchens and done with you. It was humiliating to be forced to take a position in the kitchens, but I'm finally about to get the recognition and admiration I deserve."

She wrenched her arm free and stormed away.

CHAPTER 4

$\mathcal{I}$ hurried after her but paused when I caught sight of my dress. I could hardly go to the ball trailing soot. I'd be stopped before I ever got in. But I had to warn Stefan somehow.

Stefan. Lord Westruther.

I sat down hard on a nearby stool. How had everything unraveled so quickly?

My insides felt as ruined as my outside. My dreams of making a future for myself as a pastry chef were gone. And with them any lingering hopes of Stefan.

I'd spent the day telling myself that maybe things wouldn't turn out to be as dire for Stefan as he feared—that somehow he would find a way to come back to me. But Stefan was going to be an earl one day. His responsibilities were far greater than I had imagined.

All these years I'd thought that if only he felt the same way about me as I felt about him, that would be enough. But now I knew it wasn't enough and never would be. Tonight Stefan's family would choose a bride for him, and I would never see him again.

I put my head down on a nearby table and cried.

After a few minutes, the tears dried up and determination took their place. Even if I couldn't be with Stefan, I wasn't going to let Brianna ruin his life with some nefarious potion.

I looked around, hoping that one of the scullery maids might be dressed neatly enough to take a message to the ballroom for me. But strangely, the kitchens remained completely empty. Shouldn't there have been at least some other servants coming and going?

I looked down at my ruined clothes and pawed at the soot in my hair. It would take several baths to wash all the grime away, and I hated to think how long it would take to fill the tub multiple times. I could be carrying water all night. How long before they served the dessert?

My heart began to hammer, and I scanned the kitchens desperately. I was still alone.

Maybe I could throw on a cloak and keep my face down. I might be able to slip in if no one noticed me.

I stood and took a single step toward the door before I sensed I wasn't alone after all. I spun around—and my mouth dropped open.

Directly behind me, surveying the sooty mess of the kitchens with distaste, stood a completely unfamiliar woman. She could have been someone's grandmother if it wasn't for the wings.

"You're a…a…"

"Godmother. Yes, dear," she said briskly.

I continued to stare at her.

She raised her eyebrows. "Why so surprised?"

"I didn't know I had a godmother." It was the only thing I could think of to say.

"Well, you are mistreated, aren't you?" She looked at me expectantly.

"I…I suppose so."

"And deserving?"

I assumed that question was rhetorical and stayed silent.

"And you are faced with an impossible situation?"

That one was easy. I nodded.

"Well, then—here I am." She rolled up her sleeves and once again eyed the soot. "I can see why you need me."

"Thank you," I said, dazed by my good fortune.

"I can only get you to the ball." The warning was clear in her voice. "The rest is up to you. And the magic will only last until midnight, so don't forget to be gone by then."

"That's plenty of time," I said, almost crying in my delight and relief. I just needed to get there before Brianna served my dessert.

I must have blinked because suddenly the kitchen was free of ashes. I was disappointed to see I was still coated in them, however. The godmother began to circle me, frowning and tut-tutting. I watched her, wide eyed.

After a moment her expression transformed into a smile. Now it was my turn to frown. Nothing had happened.

I glanced down at myself and gasped. The soot was gone and with it my dress. Instead a magnificent blue ball gown clung to me. Cap sleeves and a fitted top belled out into a huge skirt that swished as I moved. Tiny, glittering diamonds sparkled from the embroidery as if the dress itself were magic.

It was the most magnificent garment I'd ever seen and looked far more expensive than Brianna's gown. I reached up and touched elaborate curls, arranged on the top of my head with what felt like a string of pearls threaded through them.

When I turned back to look at the godmother, she was grinning at me.

"Like it?"

"It's more beautiful than anything I ever imagined." I shook my head in wonder.

The godmother cocked her head to one side. "It is one of my better creations if I do say so myself. You're just missing two things."

I couldn't imagine what else I could need.

She reached into a small bag and pulled out a delicate blue mask. Studded with the same tiny diamonds as the dress, elegant ribbons dangled from its sides, providing a means for me to secure it to my head. She gestured for me to come closer and tied it over my eyes and nose. Thankfully I could still see clearly.

It itched a little, and I wriggled my nose and sneezed loudly.

"None of that," said the godmother. "It ruins the effect."

I laughed.

She reached down into the bag again and pulled out two perfect glass slippers.

I stepped backward and held up both hands.

"Oh, no, no, no," I said. "I couldn't possibly wear those. I need to be able to move quickly."

The godmother glared at me. "These won't disappear at midnight, you know. They're a gift. I thought you deserved something extra special."

Guilt immediately gripped me for being so churlish, but the trepidation didn't abate. I continued to shake my head, but she ignored me. And when she knelt down to put them on my feet herself, I could hardly push her away. Reluctantly I slipped into them.

To my surprise, they were soft and pliable, and fit as if they'd been molded to my exact size. I held out one foot to examine it. It still looked like glass. I reached down and tapped against it with a fingernail. It felt like glass to my fingers, but to my foot it felt like the most comfortable shoe I'd ever worn.

I looked back up to express my amazement, but my godmother was gone. And I hadn't even thanked her. I looked around a little wildly, but there was no sign of her anywhere in the now silent kitchens.

I hesitated for a moment and then remembered that I didn't have any time to lose. I raced for the door.

It took forever to make my way through the corridors of the palace, although I was moving at an undignified pace. I only let myself slow down when I neared the entrance to the ballroom. Hundreds of candles lit a wide corridor lined with footmen. I scanned their faces looking for Stefan before I remembered.

I kept waiting for someone to yell *impostor* and stop me, but the corridor was filled with the normal sounds you might expect to filter out of a ball, nothing more. I started to let out a breath, my eyes skating over the row of footmen, only for my gaze to catch on one of them. He openly stared back.

His eyes tightened, and he gestured sharply for me to approach his position to one side of the long hall. My steps faltered, and I glanced toward the door to the ballroom. Should I ignore him and run for it?

But so far he seemed the only one interested in me, and I didn't yet know what had caught his attention. If I made a scene, I might end up with them all accosting me.

Reluctantly I joined him, frowning a question and wondering if a true guest would have responded to the summons of a footman. Perhaps my acquiescence was as condemning as any attempt to ignore him might have been.

I remembered that my mask obscured half my face and forced myself to voice my question.

"Is there a problem?" I kept my voice low and as steady as I could make it.

"Certainly not, Your Ladyship." He took two steps away as he spoke, down a side corridor that branched off the main hall adjacent to his position.

His voice was quiet, hard to hear, and without thought I stepped forward after him, straining to catch his words. A second later I realized my mistake, but it was already too late.

As soon as we had both stepped out of the main corridor, he sprang forward and yanked me hard by the arm, pulling me further down the dimly lit side hall. The surprise caught me off guard, and I barely kept my feet, the glass of my slippers clinking strangely against the stone floor.

Abruptly, he stopped and pushed me against a wall, well away from the bright lights that led to the ball. I opened my mouth to suck in a breath, ready to scream loudly, but his next words made me let it out again in a soft gasp.

"Are you sure you want to do that, *Hanna?*"

"I…"

He waited, one eyebrow raised, and I ground my teeth together. I recognized him now. Justin. Apparently all those hours spent staring at me in the kitchens had given him too great a familiarity with my appearance.

"I don't know where you got that dress," he said. "But there's no way you could have bought it."

"I didn't steal it," I snapped.

"Then why are you wearing a mask?" he asked. "I've heard all the maids down in the kitchens talking. And I've spent enough time down there to recognize you, even through your disguise. Did you think you could pretend to be someone else for a night?"

"What I'm doing here is none of your business." I glared at him. "I didn't steal this dress, and I'm not hurting anyone."

"I'm sorry, Hanna," he said. But if there was any true apology in his voice, it was only the faintest trace. "It strikes me that Brianna might feel differently on the matter, and she also might feel a sense of obligation to anyone who keeps you away from the ball tonight."

I stared at him. "Surely you've seen enough of Brianna to know that she would never give you a second look—not seriously. She values herself far too highly."

Justin frowned at me for a moment before his brow cleared. "Romantically, you mean?" He chuckled. "I'm not such a fool. But it so happens that her father is looking for a new butler. Opportunities like that don't come up every day."

He shot me a slightly disgusted look. "Oh, relax. I'm not going to hurt you. Just keep you well away from Brianna. No real harm done to anyone, and potentially a great deal of good to me."

I shook my head urgently. "No, you don't understand. There will be harm done…" My voice trailed away as I realized I couldn't risk explaining my true purpose at the ball. It would only fuel his desire to keep me away. With information like that to hold over Brianna, he could ensure his rapid ascension in her family's household.

But if I screamed for help, he would no doubt expose my identity. There would be a great many questions, and no one would be likely to usher me into the ball to speak to the earl's son.

Making a split-second decision, I pushed off from the wall, attempting to dart past him toward the main corridor. His arm shot out and caught me around the waist, swinging me back around and slamming my back against the wall.

I gasped for breath, struggling to fill my lungs, as spots swam in the dim light around me. I couldn't do this. I was just a pastry chef's apprentice. I had no place at a ball or fighting in a back corridor. I should be down in the kitchens where I belonged.

"None of that now," Justin said, almost indulgently, as I continued to gasp.

One heartbeat passed and then another. Stefan's face swam before my eyes. He was at the ball even now, unaware of the danger coming for him.

My breath returned, shuddering gratefully into my lungs. And with it came a fiery determination. Justin might dismiss me as unimportant and worthless, but if I believed him, I was just proving Stefan's fears right. I didn't accept my situation in the kitchens because I deserved to be under Master Girard or Brianna's heel. I chose to be there because the rest of the kitchen community had accepted me when I arrived all those years ago, scared and alone. And I worked hard because I was an incredible baker, and I owed it to myself and to old Master Harman to become a full pastry chef. I was strong. I had endured two years with Brianna to realize my dreams, and now I would use that same strength to fight for my best friend.

My body moved without specific instruction, submerged memories springing forth to direct my muscles. My older brother had once been a new, enthusiastic guard, determined to teach his young sister how to defend herself. I had been a reluctant pupil, more interested in baking than fighting, and I had almost forgotten my old lessons. But my body remembered.

I twisted out of his hold, stepping close to him this time, instead of trying to flee. With a silent apology to the godmother, I brought my glass-slippered heel down hard on his foot. The shoe neither cracked nor shattered, and he pulled back with a muffled oath. I stepped forward again, ignoring my voluminous skirts as I kneed him between the legs.

When he dropped to the floor, I didn't hesitate. Running down the corridor, I slowed only when I reached the lighted juncture with the main passage. With a single glance back at the still-downed Justin, I stepped out and hurried toward the waiting ballroom door with my chin high in the air. I didn't look to the left or right, and if any of the other footmen noted my strange departure and return, none of them spoke to attract my attention.

I pushed through the large double doors without pausing, eager to pass beyond Justin's reach. But as soon as I found myself on the other side of them, I froze. A shallow set of stairs led down into the ballroom, and I stood alone at the top of them.

Swallowing, I looked down at my gown, to check it had made it through my altercation with Justin unharmed. It looked just as shockingly beautiful as it had when I first caught sight of it in the kitchens. A slow swell of confidence filled me. I was certainly dressed for the occasion if nothing else. I smiled.

CHAPTER 5

$\mathcal{M}$y expression faltered when the music stopped and a fanfare played. All my self-consciousness returned.

Across the room, the gold of a familiar dress caught my eye. Brianna stood next to my pastry tower, a magnificently dressed man and woman beside her. Presumably they were the earl and countess, and their position, as well as the fanfare, suggested they were about to present the centerpiece dessert. Perhaps they intended to use it as a formal recognition of the coronation in far-away Rangmere.

My arrival had been just in time then. It had also distracted most of the guests, who now stared up at me. None of the rest of them wore masks, but I was grateful for the covering as color rushed to my cheeks. This was not the quiet entrance I'd been planning.

My eyes were drawn back to Brianna in time to see her expression change from smug satisfaction to annoyance. I felt a petty satisfaction of my own. Then a rustle of movement through the crowd caught my attention.

Someone was moving toward the front of the room, and the

rest of the crowd drew back to make way. The young man who appeared looked so different in his formal suit that it took me a moment to recognize him. Stefan.

I froze. In my rush to save him, I hadn't actually thought about how it would feel to see him. His face was so familiar, but our strange surroundings reminded me that everything had changed. And yet I couldn't prevent the rush of joy at the sight of him. I braced myself, trying to push down the emotion.

He took the stairs two at a time and was bowing over my hand before I had time to get myself under control, and my heart skipped and stuttered. I thought again of my mask. Did he even recognize me?

"My Lady." He straightened back up. "That's a beautiful dress." There was wonder in his voice.

I narrowed my eyes at him. He had better not have been rushing across the room to greet a stranger in such a manner just because she wore a fancy dress and a mysterious mask.

The look he gave me in response had as much recognition as amazement, so I relaxed and returned his smile with one of my own.

"Dance with me?" He hadn't let go of my hand, and he drew me down the stairs before I had a chance to protest. I'd never danced at a ball before.

He signaled to the musicians, and the music started back up. To my relief other couples quickly joined us, providing some cover for my awkward steps.

"Relax," he breathed into my ear, "and follow my lead. Just pretend it's something easy, like baking a custard."

I laughed in spite of myself. "You know a lot about baking custards, do you?"

"I know a lot about eating them. And I know you bake incredible custards, so you must be good at it." He grinned. "And I'm good at dancing. So, like I said, just relax and follow my lead."

"You're nonsensical," I said with a slight chuckle, but I was already moving more easily. I looked up into his eyes.

"And you sell yourself short, you know," I said in a more serious tone. "You're good at a great many more things than dancing—and I'm just starting to realize I probably don't know about half of them. But I know you must be good at your role because you take your responsibilities seriously."

"And there you go." He shook his head slightly as he smiled down at me with a warmth that made me slightly giddy. "If anything could be more effective than baking at distracting you, it's thinking about others. Now you're dancing beautifully."

My steps faltered at his words, but I forced myself to relax again and realized he was right. While I had been occupied thinking of other things, my body had been flowing through the dance. I might not be capable of anything complex, but as long as I followed Stefan's steps, I wasn't embarrassing myself, either.

And once I started thinking about Stefan, it was hard to stop. His arm circled my waist, and his hand firmly clasped mine, as intoxicating as any drink I could have been offered. As long as I kept my mind off all the eyes following us, it was surprisingly easy to lose myself in his almost-embrace.

I forgot why I'd come entirely. I forgot that the dress was only borrowed and that I wasn't the sort of girl who went to balls and danced with the handsome sons of earls. I let myself slip into a dream where I belonged right here, in Stefan's arms. It was a very pleasant dream.

"You have excellent timing." Stefan's familiar voice jolted me back to reality. "Brianna was about to claim credit for that incredible pastry tower, and I was about to say something entirely unbefitting the host of such an event. You saved me from disgracing myself."

"That's why I came," I said. "To save you. But not from that."

My words broke the light-hearted mood, Stefan's body stiffening as he looked at me sharply.

"What do you mean?"

I explained Brianna's intentions, and the potion she had somehow obtained.

He stifled a curse. "A save indeed! I won't be eating or drinking another thing all night." He shuddered.

I reminded myself that my purpose was now complete and reluctantly began to pull away from him. His arms tightened around me, keeping me in the dance, and I let him. It was foolish, but I couldn't bring myself to end this moment. As long as he desired it, I would continue to dance with him. We moved across the ballroom floor for another minute in silence.

"Have you heard the news?" His conversational tone sounded slightly forced, but I appreciated his attempt to keep the moment light.

"No, what news?"

"We thought we were gathering to celebrate the coronation of Prince Konrad, but we've just had word that Konrad is dead."

"What?" I gasped, trying to comprehend the news.

Konrad couldn't be dead. He was too hard and cruel and cunning. Even when we were children. He wasn't the sort to be taken by surprise or brought low by accident. That he had enemies I could believe—but that any of them had the strength to stand against him I wouldn't have suspected.

"Yes, it's true apparently." Stefan watched me closely. "I know you spent time in the palace at Rangmeros as a child. I'm sorry if the news is a shock."

"Shocking, indeed," I said, struggling to find the right words. "But I can't say I'm sorry that…" I cut myself off, unable to actually say I was glad for another's death.

"He wouldn't have made a good king," I said instead, filling the loaded pause.

"No." Stefan's brow creased, his expression thoughtful. "There were many here in Northhelm who have been concerned about the direction of Rangmere. Perhaps we can hope now for a new understanding to grow up between our kingdoms."

I frowned. "But I don't understand. What happened? Was he ill?"

Stefan started slightly. "Oh, sorry, didn't I say? No, nothing like that. It was a little more…dramatic, from the rumors I've heard. I haven't heard the full story yet, though. With all the preparations for the ball, and—" He faltered, and I bit my lip, remembering why he had been so distracted recently.

But he spun me through another turn and recovered himself. "The ambassador sent back an official announcement about the coronation of Queen Ava, but I'm sure Their Majesties got a more complete accounting of the circumstances in the private correspondence. My parents are senior enough members of court that I'm sure they'll be told the full story once this is all over. I can let you know…" He faltered again, as if suddenly remembering we were to have no further contact after tonight.

But I was barely following what he was saying, my mind caught on the words *Queen Ava*. Even my grief at the reminder of our personal situation was overshadowed by the fresh shock. I should have realized as soon as he said Konrad was dead, but somehow it hadn't occurred to me.

"Ava!" I gasped. My childhood friend—queen.

I could picture her image as clearly as anyone before me in the ballroom. But no, it was her thirteen-year-old self I was imagining, and she no doubt looked different now—older, taller, and probably even more beautiful. She had always been beautiful. Sadness gripped me. She had also been sad and alone and under siege. I had seen the beginning of the walls her father had forced her to build, closing away her true self. Were they high and thick now, too strong to be breached? Was there any part of my old friend that still remained? And now she was a queen.

It was a strange thought. Almost as strange as dancing

through a ballroom in a beautiful gown with the man I loved. Who also happened to be a lord. I sighed.

The orchestra began a new song, but Stefan made no move to release me or to halt our movement. His earlier stumbles had rendered him silent for several beats, his eyes focused on me, as if he was trying to read my thoughts. He wasn't likely to guess them, though. I had rarely spoken of Ava in the years since I fled Rangmere.

"You'll notice that I'm carefully restraining my curiosity," he said at last. "I'm hoping such excellent self-restraint will be rewarded."

I couldn't help laughing but then quickly sobered. "It seems to me you've got more explaining to do than I have," I said, my voice quiet.

He faltered for a moment before continuing the dance.

"I'm sorry, Hanna, I really am. You were so kind and fun that first day we met, and you just assumed I was a footman. I didn't want to correct you in case it made you treat me differently. I figured you'd find out soon enough, and we would laugh about it. Only you never did. And the longer it went on, the harder it was to say anything. I was terrified I would lose you."

His hand tightened around my waist. "Of course, I've ended up losing you anyway. I don't suppose this dress means you're secretly a duchess or something?"

He looked at me hopefully.

"Unfortunately not." I shook my head. "It just means that someone powerful took pity on me. Well, on both of us, I guess."

I had discovered how far I could be pushed and remembered how to fight for myself. Whatever happened from here, the pastry chef's corner of the kitchens would look different, starting from tomorrow. But the reality of the situation between me and Stefan hadn't changed at all.

There was another moment's silence.

"Do you really have to marry a duchess?" I tried to keep my voice light without much success. "Brianna will be disappointed."

Stefan made a face. "Not a duchess, necessarily. Just someone with power or wealth or political connections." He glared over toward his parents who were watching us with interest. "I've tried talking to them, but the problem is my grandfather."

"I thought he was dead." I was sure Stefan's father couldn't be the earl if his own father was still alive.

"The other one. My mother's father." Stefan sighed. "My parents take their responsibilities toward our people extremely seriously. Our lands and the villages under our care are always well-managed and maintained. But, unfortunately, my grandfather takes a different approach. He has extensive lands in the eastern part of the kingdom, and he's neglectful of them. But he's been letting my father manage them for years now and has always said that when I get married, he'll give them to me as a wedding present. But only if he approves of my bride."

The tortured expression was back in Stefan's eyes. "I've argued about it with my parents so many times, but we can't turn our backs on all those people. They rely on us. Who knows what my grandfather would do if I don't comply? I wanted to introduce you to him—I'm sure you could win anyone over. But my parents think it's a bad idea."

Tears sprang to my eyes.

"Stefan, stop," I whispered. "Of course I understand. Earls have responsibilities, and they can't marry pastry chefs' apprentices."

He saw my tears and jerked us both to a stop in the middle of the dance floor. Reaching up he tenderly wiped the drops away.

"Forget my grandfather," he whispered into my ear. "We'll find some way around him. I can't bear to see you cry."

I shook my head, conscious even through the tears of all the curious eyes watching us.

"You know things don't work like that," I said. "How would

we find a way around him? I can't let you sacrifice all those people just for me."

"It isn't just for you, it's for us."

It was hard to resist him when he looked at me with so much love and intensity. I shook my head again, but I could feel myself weakening. And then a chime rang across the ballroom.

My eyes flew to the clock, and I clapped a hand to my mouth. Midnight!

I wrenched myself from his grip and ran toward the stairs, counting the chimes as I went. I could hear him trying to follow, but he was hampered by the crowd. Curious voices surrounded him, questioning him about my identity.

In my rush, I stumbled on the stairs, and one of my slippers flew off, bouncing down to rest on the floor. I turned to go after it just as I heard the tenth chime. I abandoned the shoe and fled down the corridor instead.

I had barely rounded the first corner when my blue gown disappeared, soot once again covering me. I paused just long enough to remove the remaining slipper and the mask. Cradling them in my arms, I ran toward my room, the tears streaming down my face.

CHAPTER 6

My guess had been right. It took three baths to remove all the ashes and cinders from my body and hair. And it took nearly as long for me to cry myself out.

I had saved Stefan, but I still faced the death of all my dreams. And most likely an unpleasant reaction to my regained assertiveness awaited me in the kitchens.

My only consolation was the mask I had worn to the ball. Justin had proved I could be recognized through the flimsy disguise, but Brianna and Master Girard wouldn't have done so. They knew the state I had been in when they left me in the kitchens, so they wouldn't even consider the possibility that the woman at the ball could have been me. And I knew Stefan would never betray me, nor would anyone else from the kitchens.

I worried briefly about Justin, but I couldn't believe he would expose me. Not when that would mean admitting he had attempted to detain me and failed. That would only turn everyone on both sides against him—not to mention the humiliation.

Sure enough, the entire kitchen staff buzzed the next morning with delighted speculation, all discussing the mysterious girl in the exquisite gown. Everyone had a guess about who she could be, but no one came close to the truth.

To my surprise, they were more interested in her identity than in the unexpected new queen of Rangmere. I couldn't get any details about what had happened to Prince Konrad, but I was dying to know how Ava had ended up on the throne. Had there been much bloodshed? Surely my parents and brother wouldn't have allowed themselves to be caught up in any violence…But it was hard to hold on to any such certainty when my brother had been Ava's personal bodyguard for years.

If he was unharmed, what did he think of the situation? Had he kept his position? Personal bodyguard to the reigning monarch was quite a promotion.

I knew such thoughts were only an attempted distraction from my own misery, but I was desperate to keep my mind away from my life in Northhelm. I was in complete disgrace with Master Girard. And, ironically, Brianna was taking out her venom toward the mystery girl on me.

Master Girard had even mentioned taking on a fourth apprentice, and I suspected he planned to cut me out of the baking all together. With Stefan out of reach, and my parents away, I had nothing but a long, lonely year of scrubbing pots and cleaning benches to look forward to.

Who would Stefan's parents pick for his bride? I quickly forced my mind back to thoughts of my newly crowned friend. I couldn't bear to cry in front of Brianna.

A sudden commotion drew my attention to the center of the kitchen. Joanne was leaning against a bench surrounded by an eager crowd. She had obviously just arrived with some fresh piece of news. I shook my head. Where did she hear it all?

She caught me looking and gestured me over.

Even Brianna drifted toward the group, although she pretended to be occupied with something else.

"Have you heard?" Joanne asked. Her eyes were shining, so I

assumed the news was something big. She continued without waiting for my reply.

"The mystery girl left one of her shoes at the ball. Lord Westruther picked it up, and now he's vowing that he won't marry any girl but the one who fits the slipper. One of the footmen saw it too—and it was made of glass!"

For a moment I thought the gasp was mine. But it had actually come from a number of other throats—including Brianna's, I was fairly sure.

"He's going through the whole palace, trying it on every girl." One of the other scullery maids took up the story. "Apparently he's on his way to the kitchens now!"

The gasp was even more widespread this time, and most of the girls dispersed to examine their appearance in any reflective surface they could find. I remained still.

What game was Stefan playing? I'd told him last night that he had to let us go.

"What does his family think about it?" I asked.

"That's the strangest part of all." Joanne—who seemed disappointed at having lost a large part of her audience—latched on to my interest. "Apparently they've found out the mystery girl's identity."

"What?" My exclamation was loud enough to draw the crowd back in, but I kept my eyes fixed on Joanne's face.

"Apparently she's royalty from Rangmere. A princess, I believe. But she's incognito, hiding in the palace somewhere. No one knows exactly who she is. Isn't it romantic?" Joanne sighed.

I paled.

What sort of lies had Stefan told his family? Disaster loomed over us—I could feel it bearing down. I would hide in my room. If Stefan couldn't find me, he couldn't make me try on the slipper. I whirled toward the door just as a number of footmen entered.

Turning, I ran the other way instead. Blindly taking the first opening I encountered, I ended up in the pantry. Easing the doors closed behind me, I peered out through the crack. Sure enough, Stefan had entered the kitchen with a large entourage. A footman carried my slipper on a small red cushion. I rolled my eyes at all the pomp.

Stefan was peering around and looked disappointed when he couldn't spot me. I'd only just made it into hiding in time.

Brianna rushed forward, but I couldn't hear their conversation. Stefan looked displeased, but he gestured her into a chair anyway and knelt down to try the slipper on her foot. I held my breath while he attempted to wrestle it on. Only when he gave up, did I breathe again. It would be just my luck if Brianna had the same size foot as me.

Brianna looked outraged, but she could hardly make a scene in front of Stefan and his attendants. She surreptitiously glanced around the kitchens, and I thought I detected relief on her face when she found no sight of me.

Slowly each of the other girls came forward and tried on the slipper. There were plenty of blushes and giggles, but no one fit into the shoe. I glanced down at my feet. I'd never realized they were particularly small. Was this strange uncooperativeness from the shoe more of the godmother's doing?

When the last girl had tried and failed, Stefan looked around hopefully.

"Are there any other girls in the kitchens?" he asked, his voice loud enough for me to hear in my hiding place.

I knew he was talking to me, but I refused to come out.

"No, that's everyone." Brianna was quick to speak, and the man who looked like Stefan's steward began to usher the group out.

Stefan resisted his efforts, dropping behind the rest of them. Even so, he was nearly out the door when Talia spoke up.

"Where's Hanna?" she asked. "Hanna hasn't tried it on. And she's even from Rangmere."

The other scullery maids took up the cry, and Stefan quickly returned to his place beside the chair. Slowly the rest of his attendants trickled back in.

The maids, meanwhile, had spread out around the kitchens, single-mindedly searching for me. Several of the footmen joined them, and a swirling feeling of tension sprung to life in my stomach as I recognized Justin.

Somehow, inevitably, his head swung toward my pantry, and he approached on swift steps. He pulled the doors open, careful not to let them swing wide, and looked inside with a passive expression.

"No girls hiding in here," he said, his eyes locked with mine.

For a half-second, relief filled me. I had escaped my well-meaning friends.

But the sight of him sent a surge of defiance through me. I had two options: to go out and face the situation or continue to cower in here. Remaining in the pantry meant doing what Brianna so clearly wanted, and that didn't sit right with me. Not when Stefan—my true friend—was standing out there, asking me to trust him.

It might be a terrible idea, but at least he was fighting for us. I had been willing to fight for my future in baking. And I had been willing to literally fight Justin for Stefan's sake the night before. Could I really do less now? Just go back to accepting whatever was thrown at me? Or was I finished hiding away and hoping to get by unnoticed? If nothing else, I could stand at Stefan's side for whatever disaster was currently unfolding.

Defiantly, my eyes still on Justin, I stepped toward the pantry doors, thrusting my way past him.

"Actually, I am here. But I don't want to..." I trailed off at the sight of Stefan's blinding smile. He raced over to grip my hand tightly and tug me back toward the seat.

"Stefan, don't do this," I whispered, making one last attempt to return some sanity to the situation. "You know I'm not royalty!"

"Aren't you?" His voice was so light and happy, and his face so beloved, that I was already melting.

"Stefan! You know I'm not."

"Well, that's the funny thing." The smile was still firmly on his face. "It seems my grandfather was visited by a godmother. She told him that the mystery girl from the ball is the sister of the new king of Rangmere. She wouldn't give him a name, she just said to find the one who fits the slipper. So now I've been given an entourage and told to try it on every girl I see until we can discover the right one. I thought the kitchens would be as good a place to start looking as any."

I could see the suppressed laughter in his eyes as he continued. "It turns out Grandfather is very interested in a marriage alliance with such close ties to the Rangmeran crown. Especially an alliance that's approved by a godmother."

"But…but…that makes no sense. Rangmere has a queen, not a king."

I couldn't wrap my mind around his words, and I kept being distracted by his hair, which was sticking up as usual. I had to stop my hand from reaching out of its own accord to straighten it.

"Rangmere has a queen *and* a king," said Stefan. "It turns out it was a combined coronation and wedding—and the new Queen Ava has married a heroic young guard named Hans. Does the name ring a bell?"

Hans was my brother's name. My brother was a guard. Ava's guard.

Stefan chuckled at my thunderstruck expression and used my distraction to remove my shoe and replace it with the glass slipper.

"It fits!" screamed Joanne. The entire kitchen staff erupted into riotous noise, but I barely heard them. I was too busy staring into Stefan's delighted face.

"The mystery woman!" Stefan announced loudly. He was clearly enjoying himself. "I've found you! Will you marry me?"

He lowered his voice. "Say yes, Hanna, or you know I'll never stop asking. Plus, how am I going to survive without your baking?"

I considered the question.

My brother was a king. Stefan had permission from his grandfather. And the shoe fit.

I looked up and smiled. "Of course I'll marry you."

Loud cheering rocked the kitchen as Stefan jumped to his feet, pulled me up into his arms, and finally—finally—pressed his lips to mine.

EPILOGUE

J nodded with satisfaction at the multi-layered cake on the bench in front of me. It had taken hours of hard work, but the result was entirely satisfying.

"Brilliant!" exclaimed a voice behind me.

I didn't turn to face Master Girard, but he stepped up beside me anyway.

"Your technique worked," I said. "Thank you for your assistance."

Stefan would have grumbled to hear me thanking the pastry chef, but I was well aware that I couldn't have completed this cake six months ago. Girard might have an unpleasant personality, but he had earned his reputation when it came to baking, and he was finally willing to share that expertise with me. Regardless of the reason, I was grateful for the tutelage. My change in status hadn't changed my desire to learn everything I could about the creation of magnificent desserts.

It turned out Girard's dislike of Rangmerans didn't extend to the relatives of royalty. Or to the future Lady Westruther. I could only be grateful the Northhelmians were willing to accept both my new-found—somewhat ambiguous—rank, and my continued presence in the kitchens. I actually had the impression my desire to complete my apprenticeship, in spite of my betrothal, had gained me acceptance in their eyes.

I had finally heard the whole story of Queen Ava's ascension, and I was still reeling from my brother's change in fortunes. The new monarchs had been quick to send their own ambassador to Northhelm, replacing the one appointed by old King Josef. And nearly her first act had been to seek me out and move me to a small suite of rooms within the section of the palace reserved for the Rangmeran diplomatic delegation.

Before I knew what was happening, she had negotiated everything with the earl and countess, and they had agreed that I was to remain with the Rangmeran ambassador until the wedding. Still in shock, I had been willing enough to accept the luxurious room upgrade but had insisted that the wedding must wait until I completed my apprenticeship. I suspected that once I was officially Lady Westruther, my baking time would be severely depleted.

Not that Stefan wished to see me stop baking entirely. Far from it. He had insisted that he was quite spoiled and could hardly bear to eat any desserts but mine now. And if I was honest, I wouldn't miss baking the staple items that the palace kitchens frequently produced in large quantities. From now on I would have to stick to feature desserts such as this cake, and I couldn't be sorry for it.

I still felt a bittersweet pang, however, as I surveyed my final creation as an apprentice. I had been through a lot in these kitchens—both good and bad—and it would be strange not to come to them every morning. I had enjoyed my final months among the other staff, now that Brianna was gone. The kitchens had been a refuge from my other lessons—the ones teaching me all the new skills I would need in my upcoming role as Lady Westruther.

I still didn't feel entirely prepared, but I couldn't wait to marry Stefan. Being with him made all the other unknowns bearable.

I had convinced him not to make any formal allegations against Brianna or Justin, even to his parents. Justin, I felt, had already received his punishment. And I knew once the earl became involved, Brianna's entire family was likely to come under disrepute, and the rest of them had never done anything to either of us. I suspected Stefan had been to see the baronet privately, however, because Brianna came to me with the most insincere of apologies two days after my betrothal was announced.

I accepted her request for forgiveness, my only stipulation that she remain with me while Stefan led two of his most trusted guards through her rooms, looking for the potion. Her family made no protest at his arrival, offering full cooperation. Brianna herself had only managed to contain her fury with great difficulty and had left a week later for her family's distant estate.

But I had seen the potion destroyed with my own eyes, and that was the only thing that mattered to me. I had everything I wanted now, and I couldn't hold any anger or bitterness toward her in my heart. I was too full of joy for that.

Stefan had talked me out of baking my own wedding cake, saying I would have too many other matters needing my attention in the final lead up to the ceremony. But he had won back my goodwill by promising to take me on an extended tour of the kingdom as a wedding trip. We would make plenty of stops so I could learn to make some of the more difficult regional dishes that I had encountered in my years in Northhelm. I suspected his ulterior motive was to ensure I fell as much in love with his kingdom as he already was himself, and I refrained from telling him that Northhelm had already stolen what parts of my heart didn't belong to him. Rangmere felt like a distant memory these days. My brother might be king there, but Northhelm had long since become my home.

In an hour I would go to meet my parents, newly returned from Rangmeros to attend my wedding. And in two short weeks, I would marry my best friend and only love. But first I was going to eat a slice of cake.

"Gather round everyone," I called, my voice slicing through the usual buzz of the kitchens. "And bring a fork."

"A fork?" Joanne bounced over, her eyes glued to the cake. "You don't mean for that?"

I grinned and nodded. "I baked it for all of you."

A hubbub broke out as everyone crowded together, and Girard looked horrified. But he didn't actually protest, so I handed him a fork of his own with a smile. When Matthew offered to slice it, I stepped back to give him room, nearly colliding with someone tall behind me.

"I see I've arrived with perfect timing," said a much loved voice.

I spun around to see that Stefan somehow already had a fork in his hand. I laughed and let him kiss me, pulling back before we scandalized anyone. I leaned against him and looked over the kitchens, smiling at the satisfied faces as they bit into my dessert. Seeing people eating my creations was my favorite part.

I glanced up at Stefan. "Everything's changing," I said softly.

He squeezed me against his side. "For the better, I hope. My grandfather has already drawn up the legal paperwork to hand over the majority of his lands to me. My father is going to teach us how to manage them. Now we can ensure our people are never neglected again. And with a heart like yours, I couldn't imagine anyone better to have by my side for that task. I can't wait for my future with you."

Someone handed him a plate with a large slice of cake.

"And not just because of this," he said with a wink at me.

I shook my head and laughed. But he was right. Our future was going to be full of sweetness and love—and whatever challenges we faced, we would face them together. And that was far more than I could have dreamed.

NOTE FROM THE AUTHOR

If you missed the story of how Hanna's brother became king of Rangmere, you can read about it in The Princess Fugitive: A Retelling of Little Red Riding Hood.

Or if you'd like to know how Rangmere reacts to the unexpected change in monarch, read Happily Ever Afters, the novella follow-up to The Princess Fugitive, featuring Sarah and Evelyn.

Thank you for taking the time to read my novelette. If you enjoyed it, please spread the word about my fairytales!

To be kept informed of my new releases, and for free extra content, including an exclusive bonus chapter of my first novel, *The Princess Companion* (Book 1 of The Four Kingdoms series), please sign up to my mailing list at www.melaniecellier.com. At my website, you'll also find an array of free extra content including a bonus short depicting Hanna's banishment from Rangmere.

ABOUT THE AUTHOR

Melanie Cellier grew up on a staple diet of books, books and more books. And although she got older, she never stopped loving children's and young adult novels.

She always wanted to write one herself, but it took three careers and three different continents before she actually managed it.

She now feels incredibly fortunate to spend her time writing from her home in Adelaide, Australia where she keeps an eye out for koalas in her backyard. Her staple diet hasn't changed much, although she's added choc mint Rooibos tea and Chicken Crimpies to the list.

She writes young adult fantasy including books in her *Spoken Mage* world, her *Mage's Influence* world, and her various *Four Kingdoms* and *Kingdoms of Legacy* series that are made up of linked stand-alone stories that retell classic fairy tales.